A Midsummer Night's Dream

Based on the Play by William Shakespeare
Adapted by Deborah Sussman Susser
and Eric Sussman Susser

SCHOLASTIC INC.

New York   Toronto   London   Auckland   Sydney
Mexico City   New Delhi   Hong Kong   Buenos Aires

Illustrations
Luc Latulippe

Developed by ONO Books in cooperation with Scholastic Inc.

ISBN 0-439-59794-3

7   8   9   10   23   12 11 10 09 08 07

Contents

Welcome to This Book

Falling in love is great, right? As long as the person you love loves you back. But that's not always the way things go.

Take this story, for example. Helena loves Demetrius. But Demetrius loves Hermia. And Hermia? She loves a guy named Lysander. He loves Hermia back, so that's good. But Hermia's father wants her to marry Demetrius instead, so that's bad.

Confused? So is everybody else—and that's what makes the story so funny.

Target Words Here are some words to help you keep track of who is in love with whom.

- **acquiesce:** to give in

  Hermia loves Lysander and won't acquiesce to her father's wishes to marry Demetrius.

- **enchant:** to cast a spell on someone

  When the fairies want to make someone fall in love, they use a magic spell to enchant them.

- **spurn:** to reject someone who loves you

  In the beginning, Hermia spurns Demetrius, and Demetrius spurns Helena.

Reader Tips Here's how to get the most out of this book.

- **Meet the Characters** Check out the characters on pages 6–7. Some are mortals (people). Others are fairies (magic creatures). Connect their names with their pictures as you read.

- **Theme** The theme is the overall message about life that the author wants to get across to the reader. Think about what happens as a result of the characters' words and actions. This is usually where you'll find the theme of the story.

Meet the Characters

This story is set in a forest in ancient Greece. But this is no ordinary forest. It's full of magic, mischief, and love!

THE MORTALS

Hermia
A young woman in love with Lysander. Her father wants her to marry Demetrius. That stinks.

Lysander
A young man who loves Hermia as much as she loves him. Awww, isn't that sweet?

Demetrius
A young man who loves Hermia, too. But Hermia doesn't love him. That stinks, too.

Helena
A young woman in love with Demetrius. She is Hermia's best friend. That could be big trouble.

THE FAIRIES

Oberon
King of the fairies.
When he and his queen
argue, he decides to teach
her a little lesson.

Titania
Queen of the fairies.
What kind of trick will
Oberon try to play on her?

Puck
A fun-loving fairy.
He lives to serve Oberon,
and to make mischief.

1

The Trouble With Love

The duke makes his orders clear.
But no one is listening.

There's an old saying, maybe you've heard it: "The course of true love never did run smooth." Those words were first spoken by a young man named Lysander, who was deeply in love with a young woman named Hermia. And Hermia loved him, too. So what did Lysander have to complain about? Well our story's just beginning, so read on.

Long ago, in the faraway land of Greece, Duke Theseus, the ruler of Athens, had just returned from defeating some powerful women warriors called Amazons. He won the war—and he lost his heart to Hippolyta, their queen. She returned to Athens with him, and they announced that they would be married.

Duke Theseus can't wait to marry his new love Hippolyta.

"It's four days until our wedding, and the time seems to pass so slowly," the duke said, sighing to his bride-to-be once they were alone.

Hippolyta took his hand. "Be patient, my love. Four days will quickly turn into nights. And those nights will be filled with dreams that will pass the time until our wedding day."

Just then, the duke's old and trusted friend, Egeus, burst through the door, dragging his daughter by the arm. Walking quickly behind them were two handsome, young noblemen, Lysander and Demetrius, trying their best to keep up. Lysander was fair-haired, and Demetrius had dark hair. And both gazed lovingly at Egeus' daughter, Hermia, a petite, dark-haired beauty.

"Greetings, Duke," Egeus said, bowing low and pulling his daughter down with him. The two young men bowed deeply, too, both trying to outdo the other till their heads touched the floor.

Heads Up!

Lysander and Demetrius both love the same person. Who is it? How can you tell?

"My lord, I am very angry with my daughter, Hermia," Egeus continued. Then he turned to the dark-haired man. "Come here, Demetrius."

Demetrius stepped forward, and Egeus pushed Hermia up next to him.

"I have agreed to let Demetrius marry Hermia," Egeus explained. He grabbed Lysander and pulled him forward. "But Lysander has won her heart, and she has agreed to marry him."

Lysander and Hermia looked ashamed, but when Egeus wasn't looking, they took each other's hands. Demetrius **scowled** at Lysander.

The duke tried not to smile. "What would you like me to do about this?"

"She is my daughter," Egeus began, turning to Hermia. Then he noticed that she was holding Lysander's hand. "What's this?" he cried, pulling their hands apart and pushing Lysander away. "As her father, I demand that she obey me and marry Demetrius!"

"What do you say to that, Hermia?" the duke said. "Demetrius is a worthy gentleman."

Hermia looked straight at the duke. "So is Lysander, my lord."

"Yes, he is, but your father has chosen Demetrius. Marry him, or marry no one."

"Then I shall never marry!" Hermia replied.

Demetrius stepped forward and held out his hand to Hermia. "Give in, sweet Hermia. Lysander, step aside and let me marry her."

Lysander swatted Demetrius' hand away and said, "You have her father's love. Why don't you marry him and let me have Hermia?"

"Enough," the duke commanded. "Either Hermia will marry Demetrius, or she will never marry. I have spoken, and that is final."

Heads Up!

The story starts with a quote about love. Now that you've read the first chapter, explain that quote in your own words.

2

Running Away

Will Hermia's friend betray her?

Left alone, Lysander and Hermia listened to the angry echo of Egeus' footsteps on the marble floor. Then Hermia ran into Lysander's arms.

"Oh, what shall we do?" she cried.

"Don't worry," Lysander said, holding her tight. "My aunt lives on the other side of the forest. We'll run away tomorrow night and be at her house by the morning. We can marry there and be together forever."

Just then, Hermia's best friend, Helena, who was as tall as Hermia was short, walked into the room. She was whistling and twirling her long, blond hair. She opened her mouth to greet Hermia, but stopped when she saw her tears.

"What's wrong, my friend?" she asked.

"Dear Helena," Hermia cried, rushing to her

and taking her hands. "My father insists that I marry Demetrius or never marry anyone."

Helena, looking angry, dropped her friend's hands and exclaimed, "You should feel lucky! You know how much I love Demetrius. Once he said he loved me, too, but since he met you, he won't even speak to me."

"It's not my fault," Hermia said gently. "I've told him many times that I don't love him, but he won't listen. Besides, you won't have to worry about me anymore. Lysander and I are running away tomorrow night."

Hermia looked back at Lysander and smiled.

Helena looked down at her small friend, feeling conflicted. Thinking that Hermia would be out of the way made her happy, but knowing that her best friend would be gone made her sad. "I just hope you two know what you're doing," she said finally.

"So do I," Hermia whispered. She laughed and embraced her friend.

Lysander stepped forward, took Helena's hand, and wished her well. "Good luck with Demetrius," he said.

Before they parted, Hermia and Lysander agreed to meet the following night outside the city walls. Then Lysander turned to Hermia and kissed her one last time.

Left alone, Helena started thinking that it wasn't right for Hermia and Lysander to be so happy if she was so unhappy. Throughout Athens, she was considered as beautiful as Hermia, but what did it matter if Demetrius didn't care for her?

Suddenly, Helena's eyes grew wide. She had an idea: If she told Demetrius about Hermia's plan to run away, then Demetrius would be grateful to Helena, and he would surely fall back in love with her again!

She picked up the hem of her long dress and ran from the chamber, calling out, "Demetrius! Demetrius, my love, I have something to tell you! Oh, where are you, my sweet darling?"

---**Heads Up!**---

Helena's plan is to tell Demetrius where Hermia and Lysander are going. What do you think he's going to do?

3

Cast of Fools

A very serious play is planned for the duke's wedding. But the actors are a joke.

At that very moment, on the other side of town, a group of workmen sat around a rough wooden table, talking loudly. They had come to the home of Quince, the carpenter, to plan a play for the duke's wedding. At the wedding, there would be a contest, and if their play was chosen, they stood to make quite a bit of money.

There was Snug, the cabinetmaker, and Flute, the **blacksmith.** There was Snout, the **tinker** who mended pots and pans, and Starveling, the **tailor.** Finally, talking the loudest and pounding his fists on the table, was Bottom, the **weaver.**

"Excuse me, everyone, please," said Quince, who was soft-spoken. But Bottom kept right on talking. "Pardon me," said Quince politely.

Finally, Quince put his hand over Bottom's mouth and shouted, "Quiet, please! QUIET!!!"

"Quince is absolutely right," Bottom said, slapping the carpenter on the back and knocking him to the floor. "Sorry about that, Quince," Bottom said.

"As I was saying," Quince continued, brushing the dust from his coat, "we are here to choose parts for our play."

"What play are we performing?" asked Snug. He had never been in a play before. In fact, none of the workmen had.

"We will be performing *The Cruel Death of Pyramus and Thisby*," Quince replied.

"Is that a **comedy**?" Bottom asked.

Quince rolled his eyes. "*Cruel Death*. Does that sound funny? It's a **tragedy**, and it's very sad. Bottom, you will play Pyramus, a young man who dies of love. Flute, you will play Thisby."

"Who's Thisby?" Flute asked, leaning forward. "Is he a brave knight who slays an angry dragon?"

"No, *she* is the lady Pyramus loves."

"Oh, please don't make me play a woman," Flute begged.

17

Bottom stood up again. "I can do it. Let me. I'll play Thisby, too."

"No," Quince said patiently, "you're playing Pyramus. Flute doesn't have a beard, so he will play Thisby. Understood?"

Everyone nodded, and Quince assigned the rest of the parts. Snug, who was going to play a lion, was a little worried. "Do you have the lion's part written down?" he asked. "I'm not very good at memorizing lines."

"You don't need to learn any lines," Quince sighed. "All you have to do is roar."

"Oh, let me play the lion," Bottom begged, making a mean face and clawing at the air.

"You must play Pyramus," Quince said, searching for a reason, "because...because Pyramus is a gentleman."

Bottom was so pleased that he finally quieted down, much to the relief of Quince.

"Now," Quince explained, "Pyramus and Thisby love each other, but their parents won't let them get married. So they agree to leave the city and meet in the forest at night.

Thisby gets there first, and while waiting for

Bottom wants to play the lion.

Pyramus, she sees a lion. She gets frightened and runs away. When Pyramus arrives, he sees the lion but no Thisby. So Pyramus mistakenly thinks that the lion has eaten his love."

The workmen all nodded together, their mouths open and their eyes wide.

"So Pyramus stabs himself with his sword for sorrow. When Thisby returns, she sees that Pyramus is wounded and dying. So she quickly stabs herself, too, and the two of them die in each other's arms. The end."

The workmen looked at Quince for a moment. Then they burst into tears.

"Oh, please," Quince said. "It's just a play."

Quince waited for the men to calm down. Then he continued, "If we practice our little play in the city, it won't be a surprise, so let's meet in the forest by moonlight. That way, no one will

Heads Up!

In what way do Pyramus and Thisby sound like Lysander and Hermia? Do you think the two stories will end the same way?

know what we're doing. I'll see you all in the forest tomorrow night."

"Tomorrow night!" the others shouted together, but Bottom's loud voice drowned out all the others, as usual.

4

A Terrible Fight

The magic is starting to fly.

Strangely enough, the night that Lysander and Hermia chose to run away from Athens was the same night that the workmen came to the forest to practice their play.

It was also the night that Oberon, the fairy king, and Titania, his queen, were having a terrible argument. It started as a small disagreement, but neither one would **acquiesce**.

The king and queen sat in separate trees, surrounded by their fairy followers. Oberon's skin shone like silver in the moonlight, and Titania's beauty made the leaves sigh.

"Say that I am right," Oberon demanded, "and I will come with you to dance invisible at Theseus' wedding."

"Not for all your kingdom," Titania replied.

"I am the king. You must obey me."

"But I am your queen. You should listen to me. If you do not, then I will fly to the other side of the forest, far away from you."

And with that, Titania and all her fairies fluttered away like a flock of birds.

"Go, if that's how you feel," Oberon called after her. "But this is not over!"

Oberon called for his faithful servant Puck, a naughty little creature. His eyes sparkled like diamonds, and he always seemed to be smiling at a joke no one else could hear. He appeared immediately on the branch below the king.

"Yes, your majesty?"

"Puck, go and fetch me that magical purple flower of love. If you rub its nectar over sleeping eyes, whoever they see first upon waking will become their own true love. I will use it to make Titania love a silly, ugly creature, and that will teach her to disobey me."

Puck bowed his head and disappeared. At that exact moment, Demetrius walked by, with Helena trailing behind him, still begging him to wait for her.

Demetrius stopped beneath Oberon's tree, but neither he nor Helena noticed the fairy king.

"Stop following me, Helena. I don't love you, and I have to find Hermia."

"But I love you, Demetrius. That's why I told you what I know. I am your own true love, and until you see that it's true, I will follow you to the ends of the world."

Demetrius rolled his eyes. "Go home now, or I'll leave you alone here in the woods to be eaten by wild beasts."

"I would rather be eaten by wild beasts than part from you."

"Enough!" Demetrius cried angrily. "I must find Hermia." And with that he ran away through the forest.

"Run as you may," Helena called after him. "I'll still follow." She took off after him.

Heads Up!

In the story, a magic flower can make people fall in love. What kind of statement do you think this makes about love?

Neither Demetrius nor Helena noticed Oberon sitting above
them in his tree.

Oberon watched Helena go. He was touched by the strength of her love for Demetrius. "Good-bye, sweet lady," Oberon whispered. "Before this night ends, the man who runs from you will crave your love."

Puck appeared suddenly next to Oberon, holding the bright purple flower the fairy king had requested.

"Thank you, Puck," Oberon said. "I know the forest **grove** where Titania sleeps. I'll brush her eyes with the juice of this flower."

Oberon took the flower, then pulled off a few petals and gave them to Puck.

"But I have just seen a beautiful young lady cruelly **spurned** by the young man she loves. Go rub the young man's eyes with the juice of these petals and make him fall in love with her. Do this and return right away."

Puck nodded, jumped in the air, clicked his heels, and disappeared.

5

A Spell Spells Trouble

Who loves whom now?

In a hidden grove deep in the heart of the forest, Titania rested on a bed of flowers. Little did she know that Oberon was waiting on the branch of an oak tree high above the grove disguised as an old hoot owl. He sat on the branch and hooted out a sleeping spell, and soon Titania fell gently into a dream-filled slumber.

With a swoop of his wings, Oberon landed next to his sleeping queen. He shook away his feathers and returned to his own shape.

Titania looked so beautiful lying there that he almost felt bad about the trick he was about to play on her. But then he remembered how stubborn she had been. He was not going to let her off so easily. He squeezed the flower's juice onto her eyes.

"What you see when you awake, take him for your own true love," he whispered.

And with those words, Oberon disappeared into the night.

A few minutes later, Lysander and Hermia entered the grove. They had been walking for hours in the dark forest and were very tired.

Stopping under the oak tree, Lysander took Hermia's hand and said, "Dear love, let's rest here tonight and wait for the comfort of the day."

Hermia agreed, and they reclined on the soft grass and fell asleep quickly not far from where Titania slept, invisible.

Puck wandered into the grove, after searching everywhere for the mortals Helena and Demetrius. He couldn't return to Oberon until he'd found the couple, but he was getting bored and wanted to go play with the other fairies.

Puck was just about to give up, when he saw Lysander and Hermia sleeping on the ground.

"What's this?" he said happily. "These must be the mortals Oberon wanted me to find."

Puck squeezed the nectar over Lysander's eyes.

Puck carefully crept up to Lysander and squeezed the nectar over his eyes.

"Now when you awake, the first lady you see will be your own true love." Puck laughed out loud and disappeared.

Heads Up!

Did Puck find the right mortals? What do you think will happen next?

6

Hermia Loses Her Love

***Puck gets the wrong man—and
Lysander dumps his true love.***

Moments after Puck left, Demetrius stormed
through the grove, still looking for Hermia. It was
so dark, and he moved so quickly, that he didn't
see her sleeping under a nearby tree.

Helena ran after him, calling as she went.
"I'll stay with you, Demetrius," she said, "even if
you kill me."

"Stop following me. I command you to stop!"
Demetrius shouted and ran away from Helena
deeper into the forest.

Helena leaned against the tree, too tired to
continue. "Oh, I must be ugly as a bear for
Demetrius to run from me like that. Hermia must
be rejoicing, wherever she is, to have such a true
love as Lysander."

Helena sat down on the grass and fell right on top of Lysander.

"What's this? Lysander? Is that you?"

Lysander opened his eyes, and the first lady he saw was Helena, looking at him. He fell instantly, madly in love.

"Fair Helena," he cried, "I would run through fire for your sake." He clutched her hand and kissed it.

Helena looked at him closely. "Lysander, whatever is the matter with you? You know I love Demetrius. And you love Hermia."

"What? Hermia? How could I love a crow when I could have a dove?"

"Why do you make fun of me?" Helena cried. "Isn't my situation sad enough without you **mocking** me?"

"But dear, sweet, kind, wonderful Helena," Lysander protested, "I *do* love you."

"Oh, I thought you were more of a gentleman." She sighed. "First Demetrius spurns me, and now you make fun of me."

And with that, Helena pulled her hand from Lysander's and ran away after Demetrius.

Lysander gazed after her, his eyes filled with love. "My love flees me, but I shall follow. How could I ever have loved Hermia? I will follow Helena, to serve her with all my might. She will be mine, and I will be her knight."

Lysander ran after Helena, leaving poor Hermia alone in the woods. Meanwhile, Hermia had a terrible dream that a large snake ate away her heart while Lysander stood there, smiling and brushing his blond hair. It scared her so much she woke up crying.

"Lysander? Lysander, where are you?" When no answer came, Hermia realized that she was entirely alone in the dark wood. Lysander had abandoned her. "Well," she said to herself, "he must be in danger. I will find him—or die trying."

Heads Up!

Puck has really messed things up. Who loves whom right now? Are there any happy couples?

7

Bottom Loses His Head

Could a queen love a donkey?

Titania was left alone, sleeping in her flowery bed, invisible still to mortals. Before long, Bottom and the workmen stumbled on the grove, looking for a place to practice their play.

"This is perfect," Quince declared with a sweep of his small arms.

"Excuse me," Bottom spoke up. "I've been thinking about the play, and I'm worried that when Pyramus draws a sword and kills himself, it will frighten the audience too much."

"That's true," said Starveling. "Bottom's performance will be terrible."

"You mean terrifying," Bottom corrected.

"Maybe we should leave the stabbing out," Starveling proposed.

"But then how will he die?" asked Quince.

"And what about the lion?" Snout added. "Won't the lion scare the audience as well?"

"Snout's right," Bottom said. "We should tell the audience before the play begins that Snug is not a real lion and that I am not really stabbing myself with a sword. We don't want to upset the duke on his wedding day."

While the workmen discussed the play, a raven watched them, perched on an oak tree. This was Puck, who had decided that Bottom would make a perfect fool for Titania to fall in love with.

When Bottom stepped behind the oak tree and prepared to walk on stage as Pyramus, Puck floated down silently beside him. With three flaps of his wings, Puck covered Bottom's head with fairy dust. In less than a moment, the weaver's head became a donkey's. Bottom felt a slight headache, but other than that, he noticed no difference at all.

"Pyramus!" Quince called.

Bottom strode into the grove, ready to recite his part. His voice heehawed, like a donkey's. "Darling Thisby," he squealed, "we will make a beautiful couple."

Back up in the tree, Puck the raven cawed with laughter, nearly falling from his branch.

The workmen took one look at Bottom's head and started screaming all at once,

"Oh, **monstrous**! Oh, strange! We're haunted!" And they took off at top speed.

"Why are you running away?" Bottom called after them. "I see what you're doing. You're trying to scare me or make me look stupid."

Bottom shook his floppy ears and swiped his enormous tongue across his flabby lips. "You will never make me look stupid," he shouted into the woods. "Try and make me look stupid, indeed!"

Suddenly Bottom realized that he was alone in the forest. He cleared his throat and started singing as loudly as he could, to show that he wasn't afraid.

"La la la, I'm as brave as I am beautiful," he sang in a heehaw voice.

Titania heard Bottom and sat up. She took one look at his donkey head, blinked her eyes, and fell instantly in love with him.

"Oh, beautiful creature," she said, becoming visible, "what angel wakes me from my bed?"

Bottom bows before Titania.

Bottom bowed so low that his donkey ears swept the ground. "Bottom the weaver, at your service. Perhaps you could help me, ma'am, and direct me back to Athens."

"Oh, but you must remain here with me. I am the fairy queen. All of nature worships me. Be my love, and my fairies will serve you."

Titania clapped her hands and four fairies appeared. They took him by his arms and legs and lifted him, with great difficulty, up into the queen's private bed.

Puck watched it all from behind the tree. He was very pleased with himself. At last he flew off to tell Oberon how well he'd done.

Heads Up!

Do you think the magic from the flower is like real love? Why or why not?

8

Fools for Love

Can Oberon sort out Puck's mess?

Oberon crouched in a tree, waiting for Puck, who appeared in an instant.

"Did you do as I told you?" asked the king.

"It was better than you could have wished for, your majesty. Your queen loves a donkey."

"Excellent." Oberon smiled. "And did you make the mortal man fall in love with the beautiful young lady?"

"Yes, my lord. I found them sleeping next to each other. When he awakes, she'll be the first thing that he sees."

"Well done."

At that moment, Hermia walked under the tree followed by Demetrius. After waking up alone, Hermia had searched the forest for Lysander, but she'd run into Demetrius instead.

Now he trotted along behind her, begging her to return with him to Athens.

"Look," Oberon said, "here is the man I told you to **enchant**."

Puck looked down at them, confused. "That is the woman, but this is not the man."

"No," Oberon corrected. "It is the man, but not the same woman."

Puck wondered if he had made a big mistake. He and Oberon listened closely to what Hermia and Demetrius were saying.

"Dear Hermia, why do you spurn the man who loves you so?"

"Because I do not love you. I love Lysander. Tell me if you have seen him. I'm afraid something terrible might have happened."

"I haven't seen Lysander, but I must confess I'm not sorry he's gone."

"I wish *you* would be gone. I must find my Lysander." And with that, Hermia pushed Demetrius to the ground and ran off.

"Well," said Demetrius to himself, "I may as well rest here and maybe she will calm down." He leaned against a tree and was soon asleep.

Oberon glared at Puck, who looked everywhere but at Oberon.

"What have you done?" Oberon demanded. "You made the wrong man fall in love. Go find the tall, blond woman—Helena—and bring her here. I'll put a spell on Demetrius and he will fall in love with her as I wished. Do you understand me this time?" asked the king sternly.

Puck jumped away, calling, "I go, I go!"

Bending down to Demetrius, Oberon squeezed the flower's juice on his eyes.

Puck reappeared suddenly and whispered, "Helena approaches with the other man, the one I bewitched. Now he begs her to love him. Shall we watch? What fools these mortals are!"

Oberon nodded. "Let's watch from the tree."

Puck rubbed his hands together. "And then two will **woo** one. That ought to be fun!"

Heads Up!

Look up the word woo *in the glossary. What do you think will happen when Demetrius wakes up?*

9

Helena vs. Hermia

Who's crying now?

Helena was so tired of Lysander declaring his love that she walked along with her hands over her ears. She stopped to rest against the trunk of a tree for a moment. Little did she know that Demetrius lay sleeping on the other side.

Lysander fell to his knees at her feet. "Why don't you believe me when I tell you I love you?" he asked. "These are real tears." He grabbed Helena's legs, weeping like a baby.

"Oh, please," Helena snapped, "just yesterday you loved Hermia."

"I was out of my mind."

"I think you're out of your mind now. Besides, I love Demetrius."

"But Demetrius loves Hermia. He doesn't love you at all," Lysander pleaded.

Hearing the argument, Demetrius woke up and peered around the tree. When he saw Helena through his newly enchanted eyes, he staggered to his feet, struck by love.

"Oh, Helena, my goddess, my perfection," he cried. "I love you more than my own life. More than anything!"

Demetrius fell to his knees and wrapped his arms around Helena's legs, just as Lysander had.

Helena looked down angrily at the two men holding her prisoner. "How can you two hate me so much that you must mock me like this? I know that you both love Hermia, so leave me alone." She tried to pull away, but they held her legs so tightly that she tumbled over into the dirt.

Lysander glared angrily at Demetrius and said, "I know you love Hermia, and I give her to you with all my heart. But you must give up Helena, who I will love until death. Now let go!" Lysander shoved his elbow into Demetrius' arm.

"You can keep Hermia," Demetrius replied. "My love for that short troll is gone. I love only fair Helena. Look, here comes your dear Hermia now." And he elbowed Lysander in the ribs.

Hermia stood above them all on a little hill, amazed. Finally she spoke. "Lysander, my love, where did you go? Are you all right?"

"I'm more than all right. As long as I can be close to Helena." And with that he grabbed one of her long legs.

Hermia didn't know what to say. Lysander had to be joking. "You can't mean what you say."

"Oh, but I do. I love her, and I can't believe I was ever in love with you, stumpy!"

While Lysander was talking to Hermia, Helena managed to kick her leg free and stood up, brushing off her dress. Then she stepped over the men and walked up to Hermia.

"Are you a part of this awful joke, too? Why are you all making fun of me?"

Hermia took a step back. Helena was very tall and looked very angry.

Heads Up!

Helena thinks everyone's making fun of her. What would you think if someone rejected you one day and loved you the next?

Now the men are fighting for Helena's love. But Hermia is not going to take it sitting down!

"Helena, I promise that I don't know what you mean," Hermia said, feeling very confused.

"Mean? You think I'm mean? You're the ones who are mean." And with that, Helena pushed Hermia to the ground.

"Lysander, help me," Hermia cried, grabbing him where he lay.

"Get away from me, you tiny acorn. How dare you come between me and my Helena?"

Hermia had heard enough. She **lunged** at Helena and began to chase her former best friend around the tree.

"You monster! Did you come in the night and steal my man's heart?" she screamed.

Helena called to Lysander and Demetrius. "Please, you may make fun of me, gentlemen, but I beg you not to let her hurt me. She may be small but she's strong for her size."

"Don't worry, my fair Helena," Lysander said. He jumped to his feet and grabbed for Hermia. "I'll protect you."

"What do you mean you'll protect her?" Demetrius demanded. He tackled Lysander. "She's mine and she loves me!"

Oberon and Puck watched from above as Demetrius and Lysander wrestled, and Hermia chased Helena around the tree. Puck giggled helplessly until tears sparkled his eyes.

"Either you made a big mistake," Oberon said at last, "or you did this mischief on purpose to amuse yourself."

"Believe me, king of shadows," Puck said, trying to control himself, "I made a terrible mistake. Though I must admit that I'm very glad that it turned out this way."

"Very well," Oberon said, "but enough of this sport. I will cast a spell of sleep upon these silly mortals. Then you will crush this herb into Lysander's eyes to take away his love for Helena. When they wake up, this whole adventure will seem like a dream, and they can return to Athens to live in love for a long, long time."

Heads Up!

Puck is enjoying all this comedy. He thinks the mortals are "fools." What makes them act so foolishly?

10

Together Again

Titania sees Bottom with new eyes.

After Puck put the young couples to sleep, he and Oberon flew to where Titania rested in her flowery bed. Bottom slept beside her on his back, snoring loudly. Titania's arms were wrapped around him as she nuzzled his snout.

Oberon shook his head. "I'm starting to feel sorry for her," he said to Puck. "Maybe it's time to release her from this spell."

Oberon whispered in his queen's ear. "Titania? Will you finally admit that I am right and you are wrong?"

"Just let me stay with my own true love and I'll agree to anything you say, Oberon," Titania murmured sleepily.

"Done!" Oberon said. "Now, my sweet queen, it's time to wake up!"

Titania took Oberon's hand and rose from her bed. "Oberon, what a strange dream I had," she said rubbing her eyes. "I thought I was in love with a donkey."

"There lies your love," said Oberon, pointing at Bottom.

Titania looked down. Bottom's big floppy ears shook when he snored.

"How awful," she shuddered.

"It's over now, my love. Call up some music. Now that you and I are together again, we will dance invisible at Duke Theseus' palace and bless it for all who are to be married there."

Titania called to her followers and ordered them to play their music.

"Puck," Oberon called, "remove this donkey head from our friend Bottom. The dawn approaches, and the time to dream is at an end."

11

Back to the City

Wedding bells ring for everyone.

Early that morning, the duke, his bride, Hippolyta, and his old friend Egeus went out for a ride on their horses through the woods. It was a lovely day, with a warm breeze blowing softly. Like a favorite song, it lifted their spirits and made them happy.

As they rode through a grove deep in the forest, the duke suddenly lifted his hand and called for the group to stop.

There before them, sleeping soundly on the soft grass, were Lysander, Hermia, Demetrius, and Helena. Demetrius had his arms wrapped around Helena, and Lysander had his arms wrapped around Hermia.

"Look, Egeus," the duke said. "Isn't this your daughter Hermia and her friends?"

"It is, my lord," Egeus replied, "but I don't know what they're doing sleeping in the woods. Hermia, wake up! Wake up, I say!"

The young couples slowly opened their eyes and looked around, confused. Seeing the duke, they immediately got to their knees and bowed before him.

"I pray you all, stand up," Theseus said with a wave of his hand. "How is it that Lysander and Demetrius, who have been so angry at each other, are now here together as friends?"

"My lord," Lysander answered, "to tell the truth, I'm not sure, but I think that Hermia and I came here together to be married."

"Enough," Egeus cried, stepping forward. "Do you see what's going on here, Demetrius? Lysander was attempting to steal Hermia from you. And yet you do nothing about it, so I will demand that he be punished by the duke!"

Heads Up!

Do you think Demetrius is still angry at Lysander? Why or why not?

Now Helena has her Demetrius, and Hermia has her Lysander.

"Excuse me, sir," Demetrius said, addressing the duke. "Though it's true that I came here last night to find Hermia, now in the light of the warm morning sun, I find that my love for her has melted like the snow. My heart belongs to my one true love, Helena, if she will still have me. And I promise from now on to remain true to her."

Helena cried with joy and flew into Demetrius' arms. Lysander and Hermia took each other's hands, smiling happily.

Theseus smiled down on the two couples. "Fair lovers, you are lucky to have found each other. You shall be married alongside us this very afternoon. And after the ceremony, all of Athens will celebrate this happy day. Come, we will return to the city to prepare."

And with that, Theseus and the others rode away. Lysander, Hermia, Demetrius, and Helena stood there for a moment, amazed. The entire night seemed like a dream.

"Well, what are we waiting for?" Demetrius asked. "Let's follow them."

They shook the sleep from their minds and, arm in arm, returned to the city.

─Heads Up!─
What kind of ruler is Theseus? Is he strict or kind?

12

All's Well That Ends Well

Even Bottom gets a chance to shine.

This midsummer night's dream has come to an end. Theseus married his Hippolyta, Lysander his Hermia, and Demetrius his Helena. The people of Athens still talk about the wonderful celebrations that followed the ceremony.

More than anything else, the duke and his friends enjoyed the workmen's play, *The Cruel Death of Pyramus and Thisby*. Bottom returned just in time to take the stage. All his friends were very happy to see that, while he had lost his head for a time, he had gotten it back again.

When the play went on, Bottom's acting made the audience weep. Whether with sadness or with laughter, Bottom couldn't tell. Snug the lion couldn't remember his one line and forgot to roar, just as he'd feared. The sad tragedy of Pyramus and his Thisby became a most happy comedy. The duke was so pleased that he gave all the workmen jobs at the palace.

At midnight, when the party had ended and the mortals had all gone to bed, the fairies began their own celebration. Led by Oberon and Titania, with Puck at their side, they danced invisible, sang until the break of day, and blessed everyone in the palace with sweet peace.

Meet the Author

William Shakespeare

(1564–1616)

What do you think when you hear the name Shakespeare? Serious? Boring? Impossible to understand? That's not how it always was.

Plays like *A Midsummer Night's Dream* were the main entertainment four hundred years ago. Without TV or movies, going to the theater was what most people did for fun. In England, the most popular playwright of all was Shakespeare.

His plays could turn into pretty rowdy affairs. The audience didn't sit politely and watch. People talked, ate, and drank. Sometimes they even jumped up on stage and joined in the action. If they saw something they didn't like, they booed and threw things, like rotten fruit and vegetables.

Today, William Shakespeare is considered one of the greatest writers who ever lived. If you can look past the old-fashioned words, you'll see a lot of it is just good old-fashioned fun.

Glossary

acquiesce *(verb)* to give in (p. 22)

blacksmith *(noun)* someone who makes things out of iron, like horseshoes (p. 16)

comedy *(noun)* a funny story that ends happily, usually with people getting married (p.17)

enchant *(verb)* to cast a spell (p. 39)

grove *(noun)* a small clearing in the woods (p. 26)

lunge *(verb)* to make a diving grab (p. 45)

mock *(verb)* to tease or make fun (p. 31)

monstrous *(adjective)* horrible and scary (p. 35)

scowl *(verb)* to frown in an angry way (p. 11)

spurn *(verb)* to reject one who loves you (p. 26)

tailor *(noun)* someone who sews clothes (p. 16)

tinker *(noun)* someone who fixes metal (p. 16)

tragedy *(noun)* a serious story that ends sadly, often in death (p. 17)

weaver *(noun)* someone who makes cloth (p. 16)

woo *(verb)* to try to make someone fall in love with you (p. 40)